# T'was the Mice Before Christmas

by
Diana Kanan

Illustrated by Chiara Corradett

DLK Publishing

825 N. Gould St.

Owosso, MI  48867

ISBN 978-1-7330834-2-3

# Dedication

To all the friendly mice who tried to share our family's comfortable, cozy space, (and treats) especially on Christmas Eve.

Twas the mice before Christmas,

with everyone sleeping,

that stirred in the walls

before they came creeping.


They first climbed the stockings

which hung with great care

in hopes they'd find goodies

or candies to share.

With noses held high

and whiskers a twitchin',

aromas now led them

straight into the kitchen.


Scratching and sniffing

each corner and crack,

looking for crumbs

to make a night snack.

With family all nestled

upstairs fast asleep,

the mice headed up,

without making a peep.


For children were known

to leave yummy food trails.

Their bedrooms were sure

to hold treats to unveil.

The mice checked the hampers,

then trash bins and drawers,

surprised they were empty...

so, they searched once more.


They crawled up their blankets,

snuck under their sheets

to tickle the toesies

of little one's feet.

When then from outside

there sounded a cladder

which startled the mice

and made them all scatter.


They made a quick dash

for a crack in the floor,

then slid down a cord

leading to their mouse door.

They quietly waited,

then peeked out to see

a white bearded man

standing next to the tree.


Dressed all in red

from his head to his toes;

His rosy red cheeks

even matched his red nose.

He emptied his bag

overflowing with gifts.

The mice quickly realized,

he must be St. Nick!


When he had finished,

St. Nick took a seat

then spotted a plate

with a note and a treat.

"More milk and cookies?"

Then came a long sigh.

His belly was full,

but still he should try.


He took a small nibble,

washed down a quick drink

then turned to the mice,

and gave them a wink.

"Merry Christmas" he whispered

with a nod to the mice.

"You don't look so naughty. . .

I bet you're all nice."


He set the plate down

as he left for the door.

"Merry Christmas to all . . .

and, no crumbs on the floor!"

# A Word From the Author

I hope you enjoyed *T'was the Mice Before Christmas* as much as I enjoyed writing it. Christmas is such a magical time of year, fueling imaginations for generations. Even the smallest of creatures have a story to share.

# Author's Bookshelf

Author of *Poky, the Turtle Patrol*, Diana is dedicated to creating stories that are, not only entertaining, but also help to bring awareness of how our use of plastics affects the world around us.

### Poky, the Turtle Patrol

### Poky, the Turtle Patrol Birthday Surprise

### The Lost Baby Elephant

### Jeremiah Was a "Bully" Frog

### Wake Up, Farm!

# Santa's Private Email

You can leave a message for Santa at his "private" email and receive your own personalized response! You will also be entered into Santa's "Holiday Giveaway" to be drawn from all messages on December 24th

www.dianakanan.com

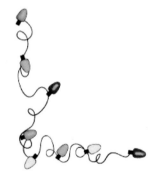

Made in the USA
Middletown, DE
11 December 2020